S0-ASW-070

PIG PIGGER PIGGEST

Rick Walton

ILLUSTRATED BY Jimmy Holder

Gibbs Smith, Publisher
Salt Lake City

ONCE UPON A TIME, there were
three pigs: a big pig named Pig, a bigger
pig named Pigger, and the biggest of the three named Piggest.

They all lived in the castle of their father, the king.

One day their father called them in. "Pig," he said, "when you were born you were a
little pig. And Pigger, you were an even littler pig. And Piggest, you were the littlest of
my dear, sweet, dirty babies. But now you are great big pigs. And this castle isn't big
enough for the four of us. It is time for you to go out and build homes of your own."

"Oh, yay!" the pigs said. "Homes of our own!" And off went Pig, Pigger, and
Piggest.

Pig found a nice, muddy spot for his castle. He formed the mud into a million bricks and began to build.

And soon he had a tall-wall, thick-brick castle of his very own.

Pigger found a nicer, muddier spot for his castle. He formed the mud into a billion bricks and began to build.

And soon he had a taller-waller, thicker-bricker castle of his very own.

Piggest found the nicest, muddiest
spot for his castle. He formed the mud
into a trillion bricks and began to build.
And soon he had the tallest-wallest,
thickest-brickest castle of all.

One day there was a knock at Pig's castle door. He opened it.
There stood Witch, who lived in the forest with her two sisters.

"Big Pig, big Pig, let me come in," Witch said. "I am rich,
and I want to buy your castle."

"Oh, go build your own," Pig said.

"I'm a witch, not a builder," Witch said. "And I must have
your castle!"

"Not by the hair on your warty-wart-wart!" Pig said, and
he slammed the door shut in Witch's face.

"Then Huff and Puff will blow your house down!"
And Witch waved her arms to the air.

SQUEAK

In came Huff and Puff. They blew, they thundered, and then they rained big drops of rain.

Soon all that was left of Pig's castle was one big mud field.

That same day there was a knock at Pigger's castle
door. He opened it. There stood Witcher, who lived in
the forest with her two sisters.

"Bigger Pigger, bigger Pigger, let me come in,"
Witcher said. "I am richer than anyone you know,
and I want to buy your castle."

"Get someone else to build you one,"
Pigger said.

"No one will build for me," Witcher
said. "So I must have your castle!"

"Not by the hair
on your nosey-nose-
nose!" Pigger said,
and he slammed
the door shut in
Witcher's face.

"Then Huffer and
Puffer will blow your house down!"
And Witcher waved her arms to the air.

-SQUEAKER

In came Huffer and Puffer. They blew, they thundered, and then they rained. Big drops of rain, then bigger drops.

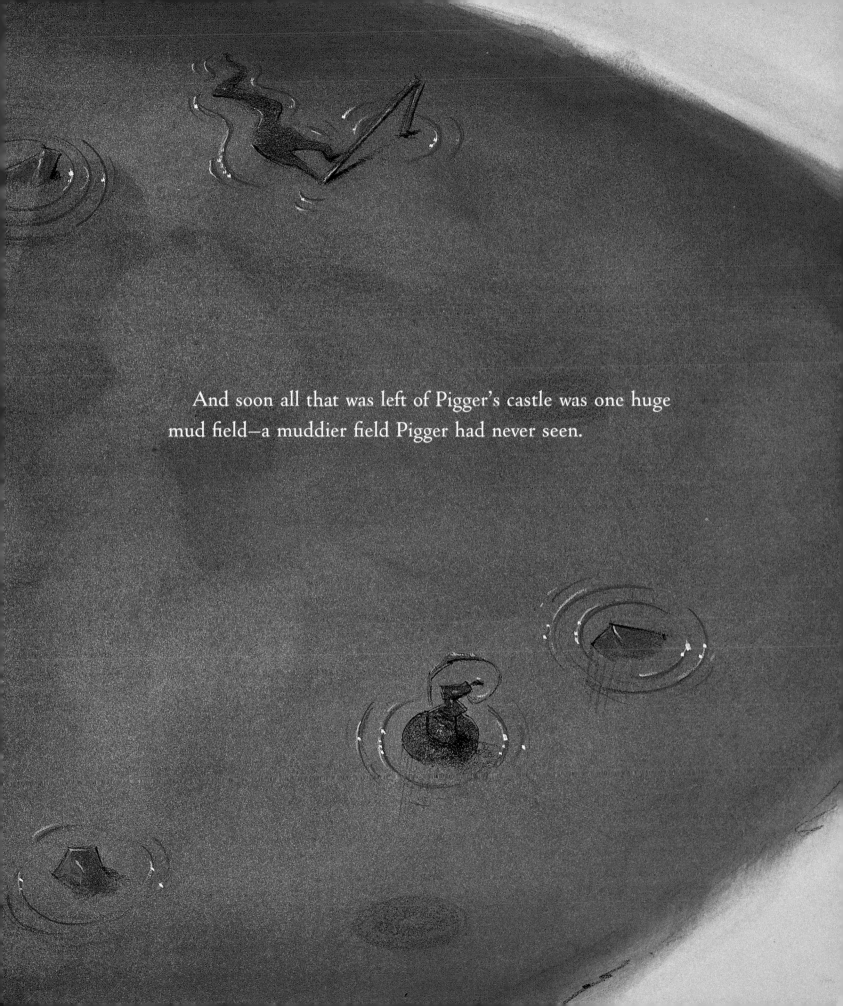

And soon all that was left of Pigger's castle was one huge
mud field—a muddier field Pigger had never seen.

That same day there was a knock at Piggest's castle door. He opened it. There stood Witchest, who lived in the forest with her two sisters.

"Biggest Piggest, biggest Piggest, let me come in," Witchest said. "I am the richest witch around, and I want to buy your castle."

"Oh, go conjure up your own," Piggest said.

"I can't. I have only one kind of magic," Witchest said. "And I must have your castle!"

"Not by the hair on your chinny-chin-chin!" Piggest said, and he slammed the door shut in Witchest's face.

"Then Huffest and Puffest will blow your house down!" And Witchest waved her arms to the air.

SQUEAKEST

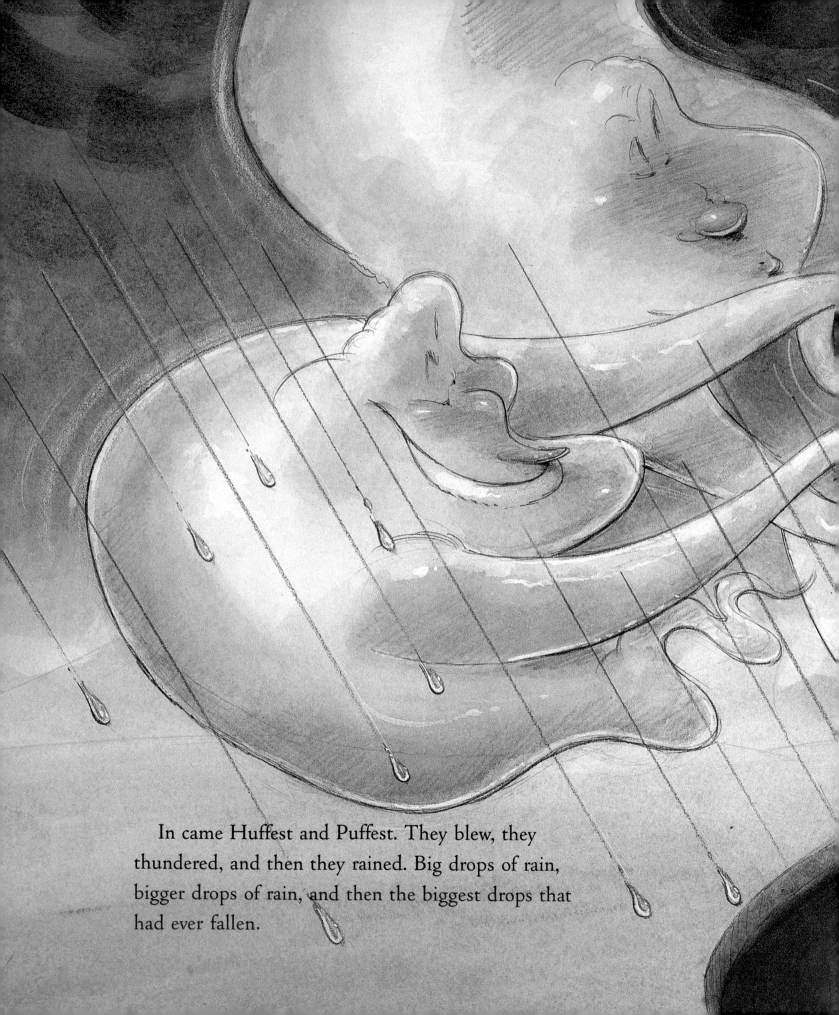

In came Huffest and Puffest. They blew, they
thundered, and then they rained. Big drops of rain,
bigger drops of rain, and then the biggest drops that
had ever fallen.

And soon all that was left of Piggest's castle was one tremendous mud field—the muddiest field Piggest had ever seen.

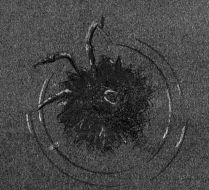

The next day, Pig, Pigger, and Piggest all happened to show up at the same time at the door of a small but very nice hut in the forest. They knocked.

The door opened slowly. "Yes?" said the witches.

"You make beautiful mud!" said Pig, Pigger, and Piggest. "And, well, we . . . we love you! You can make mud for us and we will build castles for you if you'll only marry us!"

"You want to marry us?" said the witches, as they opened the door wide. A fat tear rolled down Witch's face. A fatter tear rolled down Witcher's face. The fattest tear rolled down Witchest's face, for no one had ever loved them before.

"We do!" the pigs said. "Will you marry us?"

"Yes!" Witch said. "Yesser!" Witcher said. "Yessest!" Witchest said.

And the next day everyone turned out for the largest
and most beautiful wedding that anyone had ever seen.
And when the ceremony was over, Pig and Witch were very
happy, Pigger and Witcher couldn't have been happier, and
Piggest and Witchest were the happiest that anyone has
ever been.

And they all lived sloppily ever after.

To the superlative Joe and Debbie Ivie and their kids,
Robert, Brittnie, Brady, Brandon, Bradley, and Brooke
— R. W.

To my girls, Suzanne, Madeleine, and Sienna,
and my pig experts, Haynes and Allison
—J. H.

07 06 05   5 4 3 2

Text copyright © 1997 by Rick Walton
Illustration copyright © 1997 by Jimmy Holder

All rights reserved. No part of this book may be reproduced
by any means whatsoever, either mechanical or electronic, without permission from the publisher,
except for brief portions quoted for the purpose of review.

Published by
Gibbs Smith, Publisher
P.O. Box 667
Layton, Utah 84041

Orders: (1-800) 835-4993
www.gibbs-smith.com
Book design by Trina Stahl

Printed and bound in China

Library of Congress Cataloging-in-Publication Data
Walton, Rick
Pig, Pigger, Piggest / by Rick Walton : illustrated by Jimmy Holder. — 1st ed.
p.   cm.
Summary: When three scary witches decide they want the beautiful castles
that three pigs have built for themselves, there are surprising results.
ISBN 0-87905-806-4 (hb); ISBN 1-58685-318-X (pbk)
[1. Pigs — Fiction.   2. Witches — Fiction.]   I. Holder, Jimmy, ill.   II. Title
PZ7.W1774P1   1997
[E]—dc21   96—29810
CIP
AC